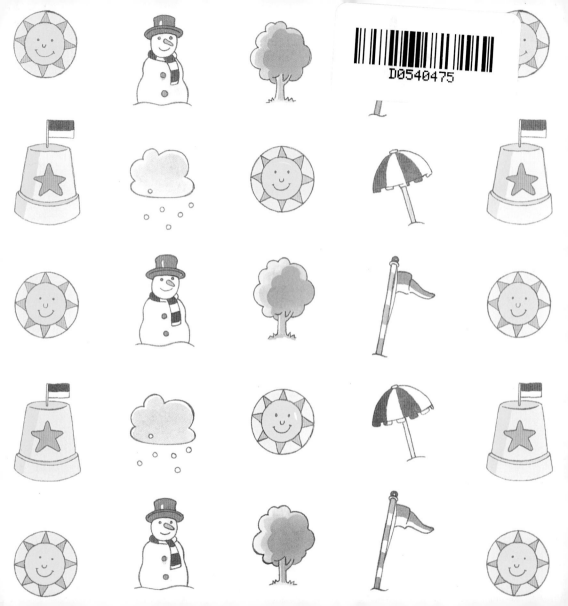

BIG BEAR
AT THE SEASIDE

Written by Dugald Steer

Illustrated by John Blackman

PARRAGON

Today is **sunny** and **warm**. Just right for a day at the seaside. Hurry up, Big Bear!

Doesn't it look wonderful!

There isn't a cloud in the sky.
Can you see the sea?

The four friends are unpacking the car. Phew! It is very **hot**.

Big Bear has an idea.

"Look out!" shouts Big Bear.
"I'm going for a swim!"

Big Bear and his friends love playing in the water.

And there's a lovely **breeze**!

It's getting really **windy**!

Quick! Catch that hat!

"Oh no!" shouts Big Bear. "Now it has started to **rain**!"

You're too big, Big Bear!

At last the **rain** has stopped. But now it is blowing a **gale**!

"Oh no!" shouts Big Bear.

"Now it has started to **snow**!"

That's not **snow**, Big Bear.
The **wind** has blown
the petals off the trees!

At last it is **sunny** again.
But I think it's time to
go home, don't you?

This is a Parragon Book.

© Parragon 1997.

Parragon
13-17 Avonbridge Trading Estate,
Atlantic Road, Avonmouth, Bristol. BS11 9QD

Produced by The Templar Company plc,
Pippbrook Mill, London Road, Dorking, Surrey RH4 1JE.
All rights reserved.
Designed by Janie Louise Hunt
Printed and bound in Italy
ISBN 0-75251-488-1